TALE OF HENRY TINSDALE

James Mitchum Oates

Author's Tranquility Press
Marietta, Georgia

James Mitchum Oates /Author's Tranquility Press
2706 Station Club Drive SW
Marietta, GA 30060
www.authorstranquilitypress.com

Publisher's Note: This is a work of fiction. Names, characters, places, and incidents are a product of the author's imagination. Locales and public names are sometimes used for atmospheric purposes. Any resemblance to actual people, living or dead, or to businesses, companies, events, institutions, or locales is completely coincidental.

Ordering Information:
Quantity sales. Special discounts are available on quantity purchases by corporations, associations, and others. For details, contact the "Special Sales Department" at the address above.

The Tale Of Henry Tinsdale / James Mitchum Oates
Hardback: 978-1-958179-24-6
Paperback: 978-1-958179-25-3
eBook: 978-1-958179-26-0

Table of Contents

Dedication 4

Introduction 6

ONE 11

TWO 18

THREE 25

FOUR 32

FIVE 38

SIX 45

SEVEN 51

EIGHT 56

NINE 61

TEN 68

ELEVEN 74

TWELVE 81

THIRTEEN 87

FOURTEEN 99

FIFTEEN 104

SIXTEEN 109

SEVENTEEN 114

EIGHTEEN 120

NINETEEN 125

TWENTY 129

TWENTY-ONE 135

TWENTY-TWO 140

TWENTY-THREE 146

TWENTY-FOUR 152

TWENTY-FIVE 158

EPILOGUE 162

AFTERWORD 163

Dedication

To you, Tamara D. Allen. I'm so glad to have known you. And a special thanks for reading and enjoying my life story. I remember once it was published and my copies for me arrived at my home. As I stood there looking and reading over bits and pieces and skimming over what I had written, I remember the ultimate and distinct feeling I felt – disappointment.

I was disappointed because I felt as if my manuscript lacked in quality. I didn't like the way it was put together or how it sounded to me. Feeling that this work that I had created was very unprofessional, I also felt as if it were a waste of time and money.

But then I remember some days later I told you that I had written my life story. You asked for a copy and seemed very eager to read it. And when you did read it, this made all the difference in the world to me. I remember that your reaction to the book was totally different than mine. Whereas I thought the book was a failure, your positive comments and just the way you loved and were fascinated with the story gave me a heartwarming reassurance.

Once I realized that I might be on to something good with this book, I began letting others read it and I started investing in it. The reaction from others that I let read the book was the same as yours – they loved it! This then gave me the spark and inspiration to write my second book. And today I am the author of eight published books. And the whole journey began with you. I just want to say thanks.

Introduction

What is life? How did we all come to be? How is it that plants give us what we need to survive and in return we do the same for them – both in perfect sync? How is it that just about everything in our neat little world compliments each other so that we may have life?

Some think that the answer in all of these mysterious questions that have plagued mankind since the beginning can be found in science. Scientists look to find answers to such inquires through physical methodologies and progressive chains of events. Then on the other hand, you have the faith-goers or those who believe in God to explain such mysteries. Those who believe in religion believe in the Almighty God and He is the reason for all of these wonderful realities. They believe that God is all-powerful, all-knowing, and all-good and that He created everything in its entirety and regulates everything to happen as it does.

Well anyone who has read my life story entitled, "Life 101 – A True Life Story," may feel a heartwarming sensation in reading about the various struggles I overcame and the obstacles that I had toppled. But if you also notice in the book, there is not much mention of God or religion as a factor in my life. There's a reason for that. The faith just wasn't there.

I had been living in the dark just turmoiling through life. However, the me now, which is a man of God, I look back on these years and reflect. I reflect on the times that God was speaking to me and I didn't open my heart to hear Him and because of that all of the missed opportunities. I am not saddened because of these missed opportunities, but only grateful that I did open my heart and hear His message when I finally did.

As I reflect, I find that the reason the faith was not there and I didn't receive God was because I was growing up to become a man of science. I would indulge in the different ideas and theories to the different questions about life from a scientifical standpoint. Not to say that people of science are close-minded, but in my journey to get where I am today, it was this train of thought that God did not exist and that all of the precious and beautiful miracles of the world had a scientific basis behind it that kept me from receiving the goodness of the Lord.

Would I say that I was wrong for it? Certainly not. Yes, I was living outside of the realms of the Lord. But it was God Himself that called me onto His path. And the fact that He did this means I was chosen to be one of His followers. It was just all in His decided timing to bring me into the light. However, there were steps that I had to take once He put the path before me in order to get where He wanted me. One of them was opening my heart to Him when He was speaking to me. I learned to listen. This is the reason that today I am a two-time college graduate and the author of eight published books, one of which is in the process of being screened by movie directors and movie producers to see if it can be made into a movie. And I have faith that it will. Trust in God from whom all blessings flow. For now, I know that God is the way, the truth, and the life.

ONE

Henry. Henry Tinsdale is a simple man. He has simple tastes in things and doesn't require much at all. He has simple needs in life and will accept the bare minimum over the extravagant at any time. Whereas most people would hurriedly take the lavish over the average, Henry would do the opposite – but for a reason. You see, Henry's is a choice lifestyle. Ever since he started studying the word of the Lord, he made the decision to live the life of a humble man.

But why?

The truth is that Henry used to have luxuries beyond luxuries. He had riches and money, women, cars, and anything else he wanted and could afford. He lived the easy life and gained such wealth the easy way. He didn't obtain this by climbing the corporate ladder and through hard work. No, not at all. Henry gained his fortune through deceit and trickery and foul play. That's right, Henry was a criminal. He lied, cheated, and stole for a living. He and a few others were running a scheme where they would look up credit card information online and steal people's money from their accounts.

Until he got caught.

One time Henry and a few of his friends were at his house looking up information to steal more money from credit cards on his computer. The feds traced the info back to Henry's computer and caught him. He got 10-15 years.

Henry went into prison with the attitude of to hell with everything and once I'm out, I'll be back doing the same thing again.

Then he met Joe.

He would see Joe very often in the cafeteria at lunch time. But Joe wouldn't be eating. He would be reading. One day Joe was reading in the cafeteria as usual when he happened to look up and see Henry looking at him. On instinct, Henry waved. Joe ignored his request for acknowledgement and looked back into and continued reading his book. Henry then decided that he wanted to know what held his attention so greatly and stroll on over there and ask him what he was reading. He stood up and began his journey to Joe's table. As he got closer and closer he could see the strain on Joe's face from the concentration on what he was reading. Finally, there Henry stood over Joe.

"Can I help you," Joe very calmly asked while still reading his book.

"Yeah, what in the world are you reading?" I asked while trying to see inside of the book.

"I'm reading the Holy Scripture."

"The Holy Scripture?"

"Yeah, the word of God. The Bible."

"Oh, is this what you're always so fixated on?"

"As a matter of fact, it is."

"I thought you were reading something important."

"And you don't think the Bible is important?"

"Not that important."

"Don't knock it till you try it. This is a very important book. You know the blessings I've received just from studying and following the word of the Lord?"

"Can't be many seeing as how you're in this place."

"So you think the Lord won't work miracles in your life if you study and follow His word. Yes, being in here is not paradise, but I can tell you I have a lot more uprisings than shortcomings, my friend. The spiritual guidance and the power of Jesus is with me every day when I wake up. And when you have Jesus, you have angels that walk with you. That's why no one has tried to harm me in any way. They see the light of Christ shine through me."

"Interesting."

"God is speaking to me now."

"What is He saying?"

"He says that you're a soul that needs salvation and redemption. He also told me to give you this," he said closing his Bible and handing it to me.

"Oh, I can't take your Bible, buddy. You expect me to believe that God wants me to take that from you?"

"I'm just the messenger."

The more I stood there, the more I felt I was being made a fool of.

So I said, "Thanks, but no thanks," and turned and walked away.

When I got back to my table, I sat down and looked back over there.

He was gone.

But the Bible was there on the table.

After lunch, I went back to my cell and left it there.

The next day at lunch, the Bible remained on the table in the exact same spot – untouched. About four days rolled around and I hadn't seen the man I encountered, just that book. Finally, I asked one of the guards as to his whereabouts. The guard told me that his name was Joe and he had been released because he served his time and got out a little earlier for good behavior. The next day at lunch, I saw the book. I got up, went over and got it and went back to my cell. There I sat staring at the cover of it.

He said I needed salvation and redemption. So if I study the word of the Lord, I'll receive just that. But what parts of the Bible do I read to get there?

Then I closed my eyes and asked God, "Where do I begin?" It was then that I opened my eyes and opened the Bible and began reading, "In the beginning, God created..."

TWO

For nights, I would sit on my cot and read the Bible. Then nights became weeks and weeks became months. Before long, I had read the entire Bible. Not only that, but I would listen to the priest who spoke at the prison on Sundays. I was following the word of the Lord.

I was becoming a man of God.

I sought redemption through the grace of the Lord and changed my heart. I spent so much time focused on the goodness of the Lord and pleasing the Lord that being in prison didn't seem as bad as it was supposed to be. Before long, time was up and I was released.

But I wasn't the same man that went in.

But now came the hard part – survival.

I had no family support, no friends, no job so that meant no money. I was making payments on the place I stayed in before going to prison, but when I did go, I was already behind on payments, so with no way to pay, my stuff got put out on the curb. I went by there to see what I could salvage, but most of it had been stolen by the homeless. What remained was of no use to me.

But through all of this I stayed strong and kept my faith strong. I sat down on the stairs leading up to the door of my old home and with my head in my hands and my head bowed and my eyes closed, I asked God what to do.

It was then I heard a voice say, "Hey, what are you doing? There's no loitering here."

I looked up to see a white man wearing denim jeans and an orange nike shirt standing there.

I then asked the man, "Sir, can you please help me? I just got out of prison and I have nothing. Do you have a few bucks to spare?"

"Now why would I give you a penny?" the man retorted. "Get a job like everyone else."

I then told him how I used to live in this place. The man then seemed somewhat startled and responded, "Oh really, I just moved in five months ago."

I then replied, "You mean you live here?"

"Yes, I do," the man said and then seemed to have an interest in hearing what I had to say. I then began with how I went to prison, but then told him how I found God and started reading the Bible and it turned my life around.

When I was done talking, the man then said, "I'm sorry I misjudged you. If you're living for the Lord, that's the only way to live."

He then reached into his pocket and fumbled for a little bit and pulled out two twenty dollar bills.

"Here's forty dollars," the man said, straightening the bills out and handing them to me.

My eyes welled up with tears as I took the money and said, "The Lord is truly good."

The man then said, "You know what...? Hold on a second. He then walked up the stairs past me and into his home. About a minute later, he came out with a bologna and cheese sandwich in a Ziploc bag, some chocolate chip cookies in another bag and a bottle of water.

But I was already gone.

I took the money and got change and went and caught the bus downtown to go and look for a job.

The first place I came upon was a factory warehouse. There were several men working on different physical tasks and I decided I would fit in just well. I walked up to the guy nearest to me and inquired about possibly getting a job.

The man then directed me to the manager's office – a little room with a wooden door with a glass frame and the light was on.

I then made my way to the office. When I got to the door, I lightly tapped on the glass frame. No one answered, so I turned the knob and stepped in. I saw a fat, bald man sitting in a chair behind a desk on the phone. When the man saw me, he said, "Yeah, spaghetti is fine. Listen, I gotta go. Love you too. Bye."

With that, he hung up and focused his attention on me standing there trying not to laugh.

The man sensing that I did in fact want to laugh replied, "Can I help you?"

I then got serious. "Yes, I need a job."

"O.K.," the man said scratching his head. "What kind of experience do you have?"

"Honestly, not much. Look, I'll be honest. I just got out of prison and I need this job. Now I don't have experience, but I'm a hard worker and I learn real fast."

"I appreciate your honesty. Today is your lucky day, you're hired."

"Wow, just like that?"

"You do want the job, don't you?"

"Yeah, definitely. When do I start?"

"Be here tomorrow at 8:15 a.m. and don't be late."

I was so excited, I turned and walked away before anything else was said.

"By the way," the man called out, "what's your name?"

I stopped and turned around.

"It's Henry."

"I'm Bill. Also starting salary is $18 an hour."

I then turned to leave.

The Lord is truly good.

THREE

Lucky for me, there was a bridge two blocks away from the factory. I journeyed the two blocks and found a nice spot underneath the bridge and spent the night there.

I slept for what seemed like two hours before I awakened. When I did awaken, I saw a man lying underneath a blanket a few feet away from where I was sleeping. I began shaking the man's shoulder.

"Mr. Excuse me, Mr."

The man grunted and groaned a little before he finally opened his eyes.

"Do you know what time it is?" I exclaimed.

"Yeah," the man replied looking at his wrist. "It's 3:47 a.m., now leave me alone."

I said, "Thanks," and stood up and made my way back to the factory. I figured I better not risk falling asleep again and waking up too late and then being late for my first day. When I got there, I was determined to stand there and wait the rest of the time until the boss showed up at 8:15 a.m.

When the boss did get there, he found me sitting on the ground slumped up against the wall sleep. He then reached down and tapped me on the shoulder. I jumped from my sleep.

"What time is it?" I exclaimed.

"It's 8:00 a.m."

I then began to apologize for falling asleep there.

"I'm sorry, Bill. It'll never happen again."

"Yeah well, at least you're on time. C'mon in," he said unlocking the door with his key.

Once we were inside, he flipped a switch on the wall to the left of him and all the lights came on. I was looking around while I followed him trying to see just what it was they did there. As I was walking and looking, I wasn't paying attention to what was in front of me, and I accidentally bumped into him.

"Oh sorry."

"It's O.K. Here you go," he said handing me a push broom. "You are the clean-up guy. It's your job to keep this place clean from head to toe. Any questions?"

"Yeah. Just what is it you do here exactly?"

"Good question. What we do here is we manufacture goods from foreign countries. So whatever goods come from the foreign countries get sent here first and it's our job to make sure it's both safe and operational before being sent to be sold."

"Oh."

"Any more questions?"

"No."

"Oh, lunch is at 12:30 p.m. You get one hour. And also you get paid every week."

"Sounds good. Just show me where the cleaning material is and I'll get started."

He then led me to a closet and opened it up. There were all types of cleaning materials from window polishers to mops, and surface cleaners.

I then announced, "I think I'll start with the windows."

"Have at it," Bill said, gesturing his hand to the open closet.

I then bent down and started rummaging through the supplies in search of window cleaner. I found a bottle that was ¼ of the way full.

"Do we have any more of this stuff?" I asked holding the bottle up and not looking behind me. When he didn't answer, I looked behind me to see him almost at the office.

"This'll have to do," I said under my breath and grabbed a few rags and stood up and closed the closet door. I then made my way to the biggest window I could find.

It was also the dirtiest.

There was a step ladder in the corner. I grabbed it, opened it up, and climbed a few steps until I was at even level with the window. Then with rags and spray bottle in hand, I began to work.

Half-way through my wiping down, I heard two voices talking loudly, and then laughter. I turned to see who it was. It was two of the other workers just now coming in.

I continued working.

Before long the factory was full of workers talking loudly.

I finally got done with the first window and moved on to the next. I was cleaning and wiping so much that time got away from me. I had half the windows done when the bell finally rang. I looked on the wall at the clock and it said 12:30 p.m. exactly. As I made my way down the step ladder, I heard a voice say, "Hey." I turned to look and saw a brown-haired gentleman wearing glasses standing there.

I took the last step down and said, "Hey," in response to him.

"I'm Simon," he said offering me his hand to shake.

"I'm Henry. I just started today."

"Oh cool. Have you met anyone else yet?"

"Just Bill."

"Oh. Well I was headed to Mr. Goodcents for lunch and I wondered if you wanted to come. I could buy you lunch."

"No thanks," I replied sensing that this might be some kind of homosexual come on. But then I thought to myself, "He's offering you a free meal. And you are very hungry."

"O.K. sure. That's very nice of you. I appreciate it."

"Alright come on."

FOUR

I purposely let him lead the way so that I could stay a few feet behind him – still leery of him. We came to the door, walked out, and walked to the side of the building. We stopped at a blue Nissan.

"This is me right here," Simon said looking at his car.

He then opened the front door and got in. I was so hungry that I wasn't worried if it was a homosexual come on anymore. I just wanted to eat! So I opened the passenger's door, and hopped in.

Simon said, "Fasten your seat belt," as he started the car up, and in ten minutes, we were at Mr. Goodcents.

We got out and went in.

When we got in, the aroma of fresh baked bread hit my nostrils.

We then walked up to the front counter to look at the menu board. The menu was displayed on the wall behind the counter. As I tried to find the cheapest thing I could so that I wouldn't seem greedy, Simon exclaimed from behind me, "Anything you want. It's on me."

I finally inquired to the person behind the counter on what was the deal of the day.

The pimple-faced, brown-haired girl, who obviously would've rathered been doing something else responded, "It's the footlong cold-cut sandwich with a bag of chips and a medium soda for $6.00."

I then replied, "That sounds wonderful. I'll have that."

Simon then piped up, "I'll have the footlong turkey bacon mozzarella melt with a bag of chips and a medium soda."

Once the girl was done ringing it up, she said, "That brings your total to $15.73." She then placed two medium cups on the counter.

Simon pulled out his wallet and opened it up and began to thumb through the bills. I saw a couple of fifties, quite a few twenties, and some tens. He finally pulled out a twenty and handed it to the girl who then hit a button on the register. The drawer flew open and she got the change and handed it to Simon. She then gave him the receipt and said, "You're ticket number twenty-six."

Simon then took the receipt, one of the cups and headed for the soda machine. I picked up my cup and followed Simon's lead. Next Simon filled his cup up about half-way full of ice and then chose Dr. Pepper. I filled my cup up with ice about one-fourth of the way and chose Sprite. We both stood there sipping our sodas through straws when the young lady announced, "Number twenty-six."

Simon then walked over and grabbed the tray on the counter. That's when I noticed an empty table next to the window. I pointed it out and we made our way over there.

When we sat down, Simon reached for his bag of Cheetos. I reached for some napkins, still holding on to my Doritos. Simon took the sandwich nearest him and unwrapped it and said, "Yep, this is mine."

I then took mine and unwrapped it and took a bite.

"So how do you like working there?" Simon asked after his second bite.

"Today's my first day, but so far it's alright. How long you been workin' there?"

"Three years now. What made you choose there to work?"

"I was in prison and when I got out, that was the best place to work for. What about you? Why'd you choose there to work?"

"A friend of mine is related to Bill and put in a good reference for me. You said you were in prison?"

"Yeah, I was doin' time for stealin' people's credit card information on-line." I saw the look on Simon's face and said, "Don't worry, all of that's behind me now. I'm a totally changed man. While in prison, I found the Lord and started studying his Word and now I'm a child of God."

Then Simon got a gleam in his eye as he replied, "You know the Lord truly does work in mysterious ways? You remember that friend that I told you about that is related to Bill that referred me to the job? Well it just so happens that she is single and she's looking for someone who truly has given their life to the Lord and walks with God. Her background is not squeaky clean either. She's never stolen credit cards on-line before, but she's had her run-ins with the law before. But the fact that you're both on the right path now and looking for something positive is a blessing within itself. You can learn from each other."

It sounded nice so I said, "O.K., what's her name and when can I meet her?"

"Her name is Debbie. I can bring her by after work tomorrow."

"That sounds nice and everything, but I have no money until payday and I have no place to stay. I mean I have nothing."

"Leave all that up to me."

FIVE

The next day at work, I was so nervous about meeting Debbie, I didn't realize that I hadn't spoken to Simon all day nor had I seen him. I had these two hundred dollars he had given me to get around until payday plus what the man at my old home had given me.

But payday was only three days away.

At lunch time, I walked up to McDonald's and got a Big Mac, a small fries, and a medium drink. I would've come out a lot better getting the combo, but because of the butterflies in my stomach, I didn't even notice it. After lunch, I walked back to the factory to finish my shift.

When I finished my shift, I looked and looked, but still no Simon.

Feeling angry and lied to, I headed for the door. When I opened the door to head out, lo and behold, there was Simon. But next to him stood a woman. No, not just any woman. She was breathtaking.

She was light-skinned which suggested that her parents were of different races. She had brown, curly hair that was not too long and not too short that came down to the top of her shoulders. Her eyes were brown and complimented her fair peach colored skin. Her figure was nice and petite. That's the way I feel a lady's figure should be.

As if it weren't bad enough that I was staring, to make matters worse, when she extended her hand and said, "I'm Debbie," I was speechless.

If there was any better way to turn a girl off, I'm sure I was doing it.

"You must be Henry," she said still pushing the conversation.

"Oh yes, I'm Henry," I replied, finally shaking her hand.

"Simon tells me you and him have been roommates now for a few weeks."

I looked at Simon who was smiling at me. "Yeah, he's a really great guy," I responded.

"Why don't you two get acquainted and get to know one another," Simon piped up.

"That sounds wonderful. Are you up for it?" Debbie said looking at me with those gorgeous eyes.

"Sure. What'd you have in mind?" I asked.

"Maybe we can get a bite to eat."

"Oh, I'm not dressed to go out to eat," I said.

"I think you look fine," she said taking my hand.

"Where'd you have in mind?" I inquired.

"Oh, just somewhere we can talk. How 'bout Burger King?"

The fact that I had a Big Mac for lunch didn't make Burger King sound too good. But I didn't tell her that.

"Burger King sounds great," I replied.

"Then it's settled," Simon chimed in. "I'll drop you guys off and Debbie call me when you're done."

We then headed to the side of the building to Simon's car.

When we got to Burger King, Debbie and I got out of the car.

Simon then said, "Have fun you two."

And then he was gone.

When we got to the door, I opened the door and held it for her like a gentleman. After she walked in, then I stepped in.

The first thing I noticed was the aroma of the flame-broiled meat. This made my mouth water like crazy.

We approached the counter.

Without looking at me, she asked, "Do you know what you want?"

"I'll have some of everything," I said trying to be charming by being funny.

I got the reaction I wanted. She giggled. Then, still without looking at me, she told the cashier, "I'll have the Jr. Whopper with cheese combo."

As he rung it in, I announced, "I'll have the Whopper with cheese combo."

After he was done ringing it up, he gave the total. I reached in my pocket and pulled some bills out. I fished for a twenty. When I found it, I put the rest back in my pocket and handed him the twenty. He hit a button on the register and his drawer flew open. Then he gave me the receipt and the change and two cups. I gave one to Debbie, we got our sodas, and found a nice table.

When our number was called, I got up, got the tray, and brought it back to our table.

With the food in front of us, we both began to indulge.

"So tell me some things about you," she said sipping her soda.

"Well, I always put God first and foremost in my life," I began. From there I talked on about the importance of God in your life and the fact that I'm a born- again Christian. But I thought it best not to say anything about how I'd been in prison. Not yet.

She listened with great interest.

When we were done, I threw our trash away and we headed for the door.

When I opened the door and looked to my left, there was Simon sitting in his car waiting.

Suddenly she said, "I did notice though that for such a resounding Christian, you made no attempt at prayer before eating."

My hands started to get sweaty. I thought to myself, "Oh my God, is this how the date is going to end?"

She saw the strain on my face and immediately responded, "But don't worry, it's not a big deal."

But I knew it was, or else she wouldn't have said anything about it.

SIX

All in all, I think Debbie had a pretty good time on our first date. Which is why I think she agreed to go out for ice cream with me on Saturday. This actually worked out perfectly because I got paid on Friday. So after work, I went to the store and bought a pair of pants and a new shirt.

Simon agreed to be our cheuffer once again.

He let me crash at his place until Saturday seeing as how I didn't have anywhere else to go.

I'm beginning to wonder about Simon.

He woke me up at ten minutes to eleven and reminded me I was meeting her at twelve.

He had some extra towels, soap and a bottle of cologne. I took a good shower, put the smell goods on, and then put on my new shirt and pants.

There I stood in front of the mirror.

"I don't know, somethin's off," I exclaimed.

"You look fine," Simon responded. "Come on, you don't want to be late."

With that, we headed for the door.

We drove to Debbie's house. When we got there, Simon honked the horn. About three minutes later, Debbie came out. From what she had on, she was obviously trying for a plain, laid back look. But her beauty masked over that plainness and made her stand out. She got in the car and we drove to Betty Rae's Ice Cream.

While in the car, about half-way there, she announced, "Is that your cologne, Henry?"

I replied, "Yes, it is."

"Oh, I just love the Aqua Velva," she said.

"A girl who knows her colognes – impressive," I responded.

In ten more minutes, we were at Betty Rae's.

Once Debbie and I got out of the car, Simon replied, "See ya soon," and then he was gone.

Debbie and I walked in.

The first thought that hit me upon entering was the vastness of the place. I thought to myself, "How could such a mere ice cream shop be so big?"

We stepped up to the counter.

I already knew what I wanted and equally she did too.

"I'll have the Buttercrunch ice cream on a sugar cone," she piped up.

"And I'll have the Chocolate Revel on a sugar cone," I immediately responded.

The sandy-haired, rosy cheeked girl rang it up and gave us our total. Once I paid, she dished the cones up and handed them to us.

We began to lick and indulge in our cones.

"So let's talk a little bit about you. I mean I don't know much about you," I said as we slowly made our way to the door to walk and eat outside. I held the door for her and we stepped outside.

"Well," she began while walking slowly, "like you, I am very much a follower of the Lord. I put God first in everything I do. But I was not always on the spiritual path. In fact, it took a lot to get me there. You see, I used to live a life doing some bad things. But then I met Simon and he really became a great positive influence in my life and helped me get right with the Lord."

"Yeah, Simon is pretty great," I interjected. "Tell me more."

"Well I used to be into conning people out of money and also prostitution."

She saw the look on my face and hurriedly replied, "But don't worry, I don't do any of those things anymore. Now I'm just living for God."

My stomach had butterflies in it as something was eating away at me telling me to tell her about my own past criminal lifestyle.

"There's something I have to tell you too," I started. "My background isn't squeaky clean either. I used to live a criminal lifestyle as well. I had friends and we would get on the internet and steal people's credit card information and take their money. I made a fortune until I got caught and sent to prison. But while I was in prison, I found God and started studying the Word. And now, I'm a changed man."

"Well Henry, I had no idea you had been to prison. This is such a shocking surprise. Why didn't you tell me?"

"I think I didn't tell you for the same reason you didn't tell me about your background. We both like each other and didn't want to lose one another by telling."

"That certainly is true. Looks like we've been holding out on each other. We have secrets that keep us distant like strangers. I'd like to get to know you, Henry – the real you. Let's try it again," she said extending her hand. "I'm Deborah Harris."

"And I'm Henry Tinsdale," I replied reaching my hand out to shake hers. "It's nice meeting you."

SEVEN

Debbie and I grew closer and closer. We went on several dates and enjoyed each one. Mostly we talked about our childhood. We found that we had a lot in common with our tastes in things. Our likes and dislikes were so similar, it was kind of weird.

Simon agreed to be our cheuffer wherever we wanted to go.

Then it happened.

I finally got my own place. I had been saving money from my checks and had been looking at apartments. I found one on Westport Road. The complex was called "The Villas." It had two bedrooms, one bathroom, a kitchen, a living room, and a patio. There was also a washer and dryer in the basement. I bought furniture and accessories and decorated the place real nice.

Simon had himself and some of his friends to help move my stuff in.

"Well this is it," Simon said flopping down on the couch.

I could tell he was tired.

"That's the last of it," he replied.

"Hey you hungry?" I asked. "I got some cold-cut sandwiches and potato salad in the fridge."

"Naw, I'll just have a cold beer."

"Alright," I said headed to the kitchen to get both of us a beer.

I came back into the living room and when I was a few feet away from Simon, I tossed him his.

"Thanks buddy," he replied.

"No, thank you for all the help. I gotta let you know, Simon, you have been a great person and friend to me since day one and I really appreciate it. Without you, I would've never met Debbie, who is wonderful. Sometimes I wonder how it is that I was so fortunate to have met you."

"The Lord is truly good."

"There is something I was wondering. I know you told me you used to be married. But you left it at that. What happened? Why aren't you still married?"

"Well, she died."

"Oh, I'm sorry to hear that, man."

"Yeah, Janet was the love of my life. And the same way you and Debbie met was the same for us. A friend introduced her to me and we started going on dates. Eventually we fell in love and moved in together. Then we got married. Somewhere down the road, we decided we wanted children. We tried and tried for a long time – but nothing. We thought it was me and that I was unable to get her pregnant. So we went to a specialist.

There we found out that it wasn't me, it was her. Her ovaries just weren't strong enough. Still determined to have children, we saw another specialist. This doctor told us that there was a new medicine on the market that had already been tested that should strengthen her ovaries, thus allowing us to have kids. We thought it was worth a shot. But sometime after she started taking the medicine, she began to complain of severe pains. We went back to the hospital two months later and they said she had cancer in her uterus. We were devastated. I went back to the doctor that prescribed the medicine for her ovaries and talked to him. But he denied that the medication was the cause of the cancer. But I knew it was. She refused all treatment and decided to put it in the hands of the Lord. Then the hard part came. Seven months later, she passed away. There was a nice ceremony for her, but her death took a toll on me. So much so, I got very depressed and quit my job. For weeks all I did was sit around the house and just cry. Until I decided that this wasn't good for me. I decided to get up and go look for a job. I was out and then on the way home, I met a girl who asked me for twenty dollars and said she was very hungry. I decided to do her one better than that and invited her to my house for a meal. She came to my house and I cooked for the both of us. We ate and talked. I enjoyed her company so much that I thought it best we keep in contact."

"Debbie..." I said almost whispering.

"Yeah, then she introduced me to Bill who got me the job and Debbie and I have been friends ever since."

"Wow."

Simon then looked at his watch. "Yeah, I better get back to my place. I figure I'll take a nap."

He stood up to head for the door.

"Simon," I said, "thanks again."

With that, he was gone.

EIGHT

Debbie and I grew quite fond of each other as our dates became more and more frequent. I would come by her house on occasion to see her, but she had only been by my place twice. I'd go over sometimes and we would have a nice home cooked meal. We would just eat and talk. One way I knew that she actually liked me was her demeanor when she was talking to me. She was always very comfortable. I learned a long time ago that if a person is uncomfortable when being around you, then usually that discomfort, more than likely, is from negative feelings toward you and is dislike.

But not with Debbie.

And I liked her as much as she liked me. She's smart, beautiful, and independent. A combination like that usually doesn't come in one package.

The only downside to Debbie is that she doesn't have a job.

But how can she have a house and such luxuries with no job?

Just so happens she has a nice sum of money that comes to her every month for social security from her dead father. Not only that, but her aunt had lots of money when she was alive and when she died, she left Debbie a huge payment.

I had been thinking about all the times I had been to her house and she had only been to my place twice. So I decided to invite her over for a third time. I invited her to watch "Independence Day" starring Will Smith with me. She happily agreed. She came over at 7:00 p.m. as promised. When she knocked on the door, I expected to see Debbie. But when I opened the door, I didn't expect to see Debbie like this. She had her hair up in a bun and it made her look even more attractive than she already was. Not only that, but she had on a white t-shirt, but it was tight and I could see the full curves of her breasts. Also she was wearing a pair of shorts, that I must say, was tight enough to turn any man on.

There I stood in awe.

"Well, can I come in?" she exclaimed.

"Y-yes, come on in," I said stuttering. "You can have a seat on the sofa," I said going into the kitchen. "The DVD is already in. I was just popping us some popcorn."

When it was done, I poured it into a big bowl, then went to the refrigerator and got out two cold cans of cream soda. Then I headed to the living room. I set the sodas and bowl of popcorn on the table. Then I sat down and took one more full look at Debbie.

"Are you ready?" she asked feeling my eyes on her body.

"Y-yeah," I replied stuttering again.

She picked the remote up and hit play.

We were eating our popcorn and drinking the sodas while watching the movie. Every now and then I would look at her, careful not to stare. About one-fourth of the way through the movie, I finally caught myself staring at her. She looked at me and I was about to look away. But it was too late; our eyes were already locked. I couldn't take anymore – I leaned in for a kiss. We locked lips in a passionate French kiss.

Then, as if in a trance, I whispered, "Do you know how beautiful you are?"

"You make me feel beautiful when I'm with you."

"Do you know how you make me feel?" I murmured still whispering.

"Why don't you show me?"

I then kissed her on the mouth again, then went down to her neck and stopped at her shoulder. Then I placed my hands on her breasts and began to suck on her neck as she moaned in delight. Then I stood up and she took my hand and stood up too. We both had the same thing in mind – the bedroom. We made our way to the bedroom, kissing the whole time. When we got in the bedroom, she said, "Are you forgetting something?"

"Nope, got it right here," I said pulling out a condom. Then I closed the door.

NINE

I awakened in the morning to see Debbie's head resting on my chest and her arm around my naked torso while she slept.

It finally happened!

I gently stroked her cheek with my finger as she awakened from her sleep.

"Good morning, beautiful," I said trying to recall just what happened last night.

"Hey handsome," she moaned. "Last night was amazing."

"Yeah, it was. Listen, how 'bout I make us some breakfast?"

"That sounds great. I'll help."

I got up and put my underwear and my robe on. Then she stood up. There she stood in all of her nakedness. I had to admire her full body for a little bit. Then I remembered exactly what happened last night. It wasn't just sex; we made love.

Then she put her panties and shorts on. Next, she slipped on her bra and her shirt.

Then we went into the kitchen.

We prepared a nice meal of scrambled eggs, toast, bacon, and coffee.

We were silent while preparing the meal and hardly spoke two words while eating.

What else was there to say?

We both knew what the other was thinking.

Could this be love?

What's the next step from here?

So I piped up, "Debbie, I was thinking we ought to move in together."

She seemed relieved that I said that and replied, "You know I was thinking the same thing?"

"We should definitely move into your place because with what I make at the warehouse combined with your money, we'd do really good."

"I agree," she said sipping the last bit of her coffee. "But what are we going to do about right now?"

I stood up and took her hand and gently kissed it. Then she stood up. "I'll show you," I said as we walked back to the bedroom.

Then we closed the door.

"You seem in awfully good spirits today," Simon remarked as I was mopping the floor at work.

"Yeah, life is pretty amazing," I chimed while still mopping the floor. "One minute you're all alone and the next minute..."

I paused.

"The next minute you're what? Go ahead and say it. Well I'll be... You're in love, you rascal."

"Yes, and it's wonderful."

"Does she know how you feel?"

"Of course. And she feels the same for me. We're moving in together."

"Oh, that's great!"

"Hey, would you mind callin' your buddies to see if they'd help us move my stuff into her place?"

"I think that can be arranged," Simon replied. "You can depend on me."

"I knew I could."

When everything was finally moved into Debbie's place, we sat back and took a moment to relax.

It was 7:35 p.m. on Sunday night.

"Well now that all the hard work is done, I think we oughta celebrate. How 'bout Red Lobster?"

Red Lobster was only two blocks down the street, then around the corner so it was within walking distance.

"Don't you want to rest? We just got done with all that work," she exclaimed.

"Oh come on."

"But…"

"But nothing, come on, honey. I'm really in the mood for some seafood."

"Henry, I'd love to, but you have to get ready for work tomorrow and it's getting late."

"Don't worry about that. Come on, we'll have a good time."

"Alright," she said standing up grabbing her door keys.

Why is he so anxious to get to Red Lobster?

We headed out the door.

As Debbie and I walked down the street hand in hand, we both felt a gentle summer breeze striking our faces as the scent of one of our neighbor's barbeque grill caught the both of our nostrils.

A perfect night to be with the one you love.

Finally, we reached Red Lobster.

When we walked in, a young lady greeted us and directed us toward a booth.

We sat and waited for a waiter for a little while. Then a little while became a long while. I could see Debbie growing impatient. Then she exclaimed, "What's taking so long? This is terrible customer service."

She then looked at me and inquired, "And what's funny?"

It was then that I realized I was smiling.

But for a reason.

I couldn't wait any longer.

Finally, I got down on one knee and pulled a pink box out of my pocket.

Debbie covered her mouth as the tears welled up in her eyes.

Then with no hesitation, I asked, "Deborah Anne Harris, will you do me the honors and make me the happiest man on the planet by marrying me?"

Then I opened the box to show her the ring.

"Oh Henry. Yes, yes I will."

TEN

We didn't want a big fancy wedding with a lot of people, so we decided to go downtown and make it legal.

Of course, we had Simon's blessing and he was there to support us anyway he could.

So, there it was; Mr. and Mrs. Tinsdale began their life together.

I loved her and she loved me. There was nothing we couldn't talk about. Although our favorite topic to talk about very often was the Bible. We would read and study and learn and grow in the word of the Lord together.

But studying and living the word wasn't enough. We found a nice church to go to every Sunday and worship.

Life was getting better and better for us.

Then on the morning of my birthday, I found out just how good Debbie could cook.

When I awakened that morning, the aroma of greatness hit my nose. In fact, it was so great that I thought it was a dream and tried to go back to sleep.

But to no avail.

The aroma was so good and strong that I had to get up and check it out. When I got to the kitchen, there I saw Debbie sitting at the table drinking a cup of coffee. Across from her, on my side of the table was a plate of hashbrowns, scrambled eggs, bacon, and toast. And in front of the plate was a cup of coffee.

I didn't waste any time taking my seat. We said grace and then I began to indulge. I ate and ate and when I was done, I sat back in content. The only thing I could think of to say was, "Where did you learn to cook like this?"

She smiled and pointed towards the kitchen sink.

There was an open book just sitting there.

A cookbook.

I was so pleased with her and just the quality of the food was so amazing that it was then and there that I told her to only cook this meal for me on special occasions exactly like that.

She agreed.

Then we celebrated my birthday.

After I opened the gifts, we decided to study the Bible more. Often I would try to explain scriptures and verses to Debbie. Although for the past few weeks, she seemed to have somewhat of a lack of interest when studying. Sometimes she would be unresponsive with little or nothing to say. Today I was trying to teach her about the sacrificial lamb.

"So the sacrificial lamb is just like the sacrificing of one of the good for the sake or betterment of others," I announced. "Honey, are you O.K.?" I asked uncertain if she was even listening. So I asked if she was listening.

"Yes, I'm listening. It's just that it's your birthday. Why do we always have to study the Bible?"

"Babe, we always study every day at this time."

"Yeah, studying the Bible is nice and all, but it gets boring. It's time to live a little."

I was shocked, but for some reason I couldn't say I didn't see it coming.

"I don't know. It's like she's growing more distant," I said to Simon about to take a bite of my sandwich.

We were having lunch at Panera Bread.

"That just doesn't sound like her," Simon responded.

"Yeah, I know. I don't want to believe it either, but it's true."

"Well just keep at it. But on a better note, Bill was telling me that he thinks that you're such a great worker, that he's gonna give you more hours. But don't tell him I told you because I think he wanted to tell you himself."

"Oh that's great."

"Well we oughta be headin' back," Simon said looking at his watch.

I shoved the last bit of sandwich in my mouth, took a sip of my soda, and we were gone.

When we got back to the warehouse, as soon as I stepped in, Bill came out of his office and approached me.

"Hey Henry, I been meaning to talk to you."

"About what?" I responded watching him walk towards me.

Finally, he was in front of me when he said, "Well you know I liked you from day one since you started here and you're a very efficient and hard worker. So I want to give you more hours and a raise. The only thing I ask is can you take a different shift for me? Can you work, say nights?"

"But I thought the warehouse was closed overnight."

"Which is why I'm giving you a key so you can come in and work and lock up when you're done. What do ya say?"

"Oh that's awesome. Just one thing, let me save up enough money to buy a car so I can get around."

"Sure thing, buddy. Now just do me one favor. The closet needs cleaning out and then you can go home early."

"Thanks Bill, for everything."

"Don't mention it."

ELEVEN

"Oh Henry, it's gorgeous," Debbie said in awe staring at the cherry red Taurus I just pulled up in.

"Let's go for a ride," she said opening the passenger door and hopping in.

"Where to?" I asked still sitting in the driver's seat.

"Anywhere, I don't care. Let's just ride."

With that, we were off.

We were driving for about five minutes in silence just enjoying the breeze when I announced, "You know, I'll be working at night now at the warehouse instead of during the day. Bill's giving me a key. And I'm getting more hours and a raise."

"That's wonderful."

"You know, this calls for a celebration. What do you think we ought to do to celebrate?"

"I can think of a few things," she said placing her hand on my leg and moving up to my thigh.

"You know I love that thing you do with the ice," I said envisioning the first time we made love.

"Anything you want," she seductively said.

"Well what are we waiting for?" I said making a U-turn at the intersection.

And then we were on our way home.

When we got to the door, Debbie walked in and I walked in behind her. She turned around to ask me a question and when she did, she walked right into a passionate kiss.

We were kissing and she tried to put her house keys on the table, but because she was so involved with the kiss, she missed the table and they fell on the floor.

We didn't care. Here we were in heat.

As we kissed, we made our way to the bedroom.

By the time we got to the bedroom, both our shirts were off.

Before I closed the door, Debbie replied, "Oh honey, don't forget the ice."

Here we lay naked cuddled up against one another. I was half-awake and half-sleep lying there thinking that life couldn't get any better than this.

Then the doorbell rang.

I slid out of bed, careful not to wake Debbie, then put on my robe and slippers and headed for the door. When I got to the living room, I saw Debbie's keys on the floor. As I bent over to pick them up, the doorbell rang again.

"I'm coming," I snapped wondering who it was disturbing my peace.

I got to the door and opened it. There stood Simon.

"Hey Henry."

"Oh hey Simon. What's up?"

"Oh I just came by to check on my two favorite people in the whole world. Can I come in for a little bit?"

"Oh yeah, buddy, you couldn't have picked a worse time. Debbie and I are pretty worn out from this morning," I said purposely leaving out the details.

"Oh, well I'll just drop by later or you two can come by my place when you're not busy."

"Sounds good."

"Alright buddy. See ya at work."

"Oh actually I don't think I'll see you at work anymore. Remember that night shift position Bill offered me? Well he was just waiting on me to get a car. Check it out," I said pointing behind him.

He turned around and then exclaimed, "Wow, that's you?"

"Yep."

He began to approach it and just stared in delight.

"What do you think?"

"Wow, it's a beauty. If I hadn't got a Nissan, then a Taurus would've been my first choice. And it's the right color. You really lucked out."

"Yeah, tell me about it."

After looking at it a few more seconds, Simon finally said, "Well I'm not gonna hold you up any longer. I better be headin' back to my place. Henry, I just wanna say I'm so proud of you. You've come a really long way."

"Yeah, you know I was just thinking about that the other day. And I know for a fact, I owe a lot of credit to you. More credit than you think. I couldn't have accomplished half this stuff without you. I just wanna say thanks."

"Oh, don't mention it, buddy. The Lord is truly good, isn't He?"

"That He is indeed."

"Speaking of our Lord, how's Debbie coming with getting back into the word? I know you told me she seems to be losing interest."

"Well it's not getting any better. She doesn't like to study as much and when we are studying, she finds a reason to stop."

"Hmmm, doesn't sound like her. Well, I'll keep her in my prayers. I got to be headin' back."

"Alright buddy, take care," I said and turned around and headed for the door.

When I came in, that aroma of greatness hit my nostrils.

She was cooking my special meal.

"Hey honey, I was thinking, maybe after we eat we can study more of the Bible."

"Oh, I don't think it's a good time for that. After we eat, we have to get a few things from the store."

She was obviously making excuses.

"Sure Deb."

TWELVE

"So how do you feel about working at night?" Debbie asked me while taking a bite of her rice. We were having Chinese fried rice and egg rolls for dinner. Tonight was my first night to start. I was to be there in an hour.

"Oh it sounds alright. I'll have the whole place to myself."

"And then when you come home, it's just me and you."

"Yeah definitely, but I'll need a few hours of sleep first."

"Of course."

Fifteen minutes later, we were done eating and decided to watch some T.V.

We were watching a movie with Kevin Costner. We were both enthralled while watching the movie. I looked over at her and she was on the edge of the couch engrossed in the film. Thirty-five minutes later, while I was still watching, I heard her snoring. I looked over to see her slumped over sleeping. I went to the bedroom and got a blanket and came back and draped it across her.

I love you, Debbie.

Then I was ready to go. I grabbed the house keys, the car keys, and the keys to the warehouse and then turned the light off and I headed for the door.

When I got to the car, I caught a cool gust of a breeze. It was a summer's breeze just hinting on fall.

Although somehow something just wasn't right.

I could feel it.

Then I thought to myself that I just must be feeling this way from excitement of working my overnight shift. I took a deep breath, unlocked the door, and hopped in.

Then I was on my way to the warehouse.

While driving, I decided not to listen to any music. But just to think. I thought about everything. I envisioned the times I had before prison with the fast money and living the high life. I thought about when I was actually in prison and all the times of studying the word and asking God to make sure no one harmed me while I was there. Then I thought about when I got out and got the job at the warehouse and meeting Simon.

God must have sent him to me. You just don't meet people that nice and friendly. Then I thought about Debbie and the way I felt when I first saw her and saw how beautiful she was. And then I thought about how distant she had grown from the Bible and the way she was forsaking the word.

The next thing I knew, I was at the warehouse.

I got out and locked the car door and used the key Bill gave me to get in.

When I got in, I turned the lights on and locked the door behind me. I went to the closet and found some surface cleaner and a rag and got busy. I took out the ear buds I bought and put them in my ears. I listened to Ice Cube. Before long I was done wiping down. So next I got the glass cleaner and polished the windows. Then I grabbed a broom and swept. When I finished that I made some mop water and got the mop and mopped the floors.

When I finished, I just stood there and marveled at my work.

Then, as if someone were there with me, I said, "That's good enough for now."

Then I turned around and headed for the door and turned the lights out and left. I locked the door behind me and went to my car.

When I got in, I sat there for a moment just to enjoy the silence. Then I started the car up and headed for home.

When I got home, I came in quietly hoping that Debbie was still sleep. When I got to the living room, she wasn't there, so I went to the bedroom. There she was curled up under the covers resting peacefully. At that point, I just wanted to get undressed and get in bed, but quietly so as not to wake her. I didn't want to wake her because I knew she would want to talk about how my night went and that's definitely what I didn't want to do. I just wanted to sleep.

So as quietly as I could, I got undressed and climbed in bed.

Before I knew it, I was sleep.

But before I finally did fall asleep, I got the weirdest notion that Debbie was awake but just fake sleeping.

Maybe she knew I was tired and she didn't want to bother me.

THIRTEEN

It became routine to work overnight, come home and get a few hours of sleep, and then spend the day with Debbie.

A lot of times she liked to go out – as opposed to studying the Bible.

One morning, I came home as usual, got in my robe and went to sleep. When I awakened, I found the bed was empty. I got up and went into the kitchen. I saw Debbie standing there brewing a pot of coffee.

"Good morning."

"Good morning, honey. How was work?"

"Oh same old, same old. Only thing is I don't know why exactly, but I'm a lot more tired this morning than usual."

"Aw, well get some more rest."

"Yeah, I was going to. I'll just brush my teeth real quick, then I'm headed back to bed."

I went to the bathroom, opened the cabinet and got my toothbrush and toothpaste out. Then I put the toothpaste on the brush and began. About thirty seconds after I started, the doorbell rang.

"I'll get it," Debbie replied from the kitchen.

I heard the front door open and then about five seconds later, Debbie yelled back to me, "It's Simon."

I rinsed my mouth and came to greet him. As I made my way to the living room, I thought to myself, "You couldn't have picked a better time than now to come over?"

"Hey buddy, how ya doin'?" I said coming into the living room to see Simon sitting on the couch.

"Hey man, how's it goin'?" Simon responded.

"Oh nothin' much. Just a little tired."

"Hey, I was thinkin' how about you, me, and Debbie goin' out today?"

"Oh, that sounds nice, but I'm really kind-of tired from last night. I was planning on getting some more rest before I have to go back in tonight."

"Aw, come on, Henry," Debbie said. "It'll be fun."

"Yeah, and I promise we'll be back in time for you to get plenty of rest," Simon replied.

Against my better judgement, I gave in and said, "O.K."

"Just let me get my clothes on real quick."

I went into the bedroom, threw on some deodorant and cologne, and my clothes and socks and shoes and I was ready.

I walked into the living room to see Simon and Debbie weren't there. But I heard muttled voices. So I walked closer. I could hear the two of them on the front porch talking.

"Well, I don't see what the problem is," I heard Debbie say.

"He's just a little concerned about you," Simon responded.

I cleared my throat to alert them of my presence.

"I'm ready," I announced.

"Alright let's go," Simon replied.

"Where to?" I inquired.

Simon then smiled and said, "It's a surprise."

Then we all got in his car and headed for the surprise.

We drove for about twenty minutes in silence when Simon finally pulled up to a building and parked in the lot.

"Gentri's Massage Parlor," I said reading the sign aloud.

"This is a great surprise," Debbie exclaimed getting out of the car.

Then me and Simon got out and we all walked in.

When we got in, I felt a certain comfort. Just the fact that the lights were low and the quietness of the place helped to relieve some tension from my body.

Then the short, curly-haired man behind the counter said, "How can I help you today?"

Although I couldn't place his accent.

"Yes, the three of us would like a full-body massage," Simon announced reaching into his back pocket. He pulled out his wallet and then pulled his credit card out.

"Alright," the man said taking Simon's credit card and swiping it, then handing it back to Simon with a receipt.

He then stepped from behind the counter and we could see him fully.

"Right this way," he said gesturing with his hand.

He led us to three different rooms; one for each one of us. In each room there was someone there waiting.

"Three full bodies," he announced to each person.

They then closed the doors and worked their magic.

The whole time I was getting my massage, I decided to put all of my worries out of my mind and just meditate. I imagined I was on an island sitting on the ocean shore while the cool water ever-so often tickled my feet.

It actually worked!

By the time my massage was over, I felt so loose and stress-free.

The only problem was that it also made me feel more tired.

When I came out of the room, Debbie and Simon were there waiting on me.

They were already done.

"How was you guys' massages?" I asked.

"Yeah, it was O.K. for what it was worth," Simon responded.

"Yeah, same here," Debbie chimed in.

"How 'bout yours?" Simon inquired.

"Oh, it was O.K. Just relieved a little tension."

For some reason, I figured I shouldn't let on as to how much better mine was than theirs.

"Where to now?" I quickly asked trying to change the subject.

"Well," Simon started, "I was thinking we could get you some music. I figure you could listen to it while you work. Just somethin' so you won't get bored."

"Oh, I actually have my tunes the whole time I'm working."

"Who do you listen to?"

"Ice Cube."

"Ice Cube...?" Simon said sarcastically. "It's time you step your game up. What about Snoop Dogg? Now he's tight. Don't you like 'Drop it like it's hot?"

"No, not really," I said playing Simon off. He could tell I was lying.

Who doesn't like Snoop Dogg and Pharell?

"Well my friend," Simon said patting me on the back, "a music makeover is about to be in session. I think Marvin Gaye said it best, "Let's get it on."

Then we headed to the car.

When we got to the mall, we headed straight to the music store.

"Alright guys, any music you want, it's on me," Simon announced.

"But Simon, you don't have to..." I replied.

"Nope," Simon said putting his finger to his lips as if shh-shhing me. "It's on me," he said again.

"Well in that case, Debbie, you take everything on this side of the room and I'll take everything on that side."

"Yeah, good luck listening to all of it," Simon teased and the two of us laughed. Simon and I joked and laughed for a few more minutes before we realized that Debbie had slipped away. I looked to my right and then further down and there she was at the opposite end of the store. Then she started to make her way back to us. She had something in hand.

"Found something already?" Simon asked.

"Yeah, just this," she said showing us her CD. It was "The Delfonics."

"I didn't know you go back that far," Simon exclaimed.

"Yeah, I'm really into Ole School."

"How 'bout you, Henry?"

I decided to choose anything just so we could hurry and get out of there. I was still very tired and there's nowhere I'd rather be right now than at home in my bed.

So I piped up, "What about the new Tupac?"

I hadn't heard that there was a new Tupac, but I figured there must be one because every so often, there would be a new one to arise.

"Wise choice, my friend," Simon said walking up to the counter. "Do you have the new Tupac?" he asked the lady working there.

"Yeah, right this way," she said stepping from behind the counter and leading the way. I could see the tattoos on her arms. She looked as if she might be part of the LGBT community.

Finally, we reached the CD rack. She looked on one entire row and then she went down to the row below it until she found it.

"Here ya go," the lady said handing it to Simon.

"Well if there's nothing else, let's get this paid for so we can get going," Simon said talking to me and Debbie.

We walked up to the counter and Simon paid for the CD's and we left. As we were coming out of the entrance, I said, "So now we're headed home," contemplating on finally getting more sleep.

"Oh, I thought we were headed for lunch now," Simon replied.

In my mind, I thought to myself, "Aw naw."

"Sounds great," I said trying not to sound tired.

But it actually showed more than I thought. The odd part is I think Simon knew exactly how tired I was.

But what were his intentions.

I don't know.

FOURTEEN

We had lunch at a pizza place, then Simon dropped me and Debbie off at home.

Words can't describe the relief I had when walking through the door and about to finally get more sleep.

"Hey honey, wanna watch a movie?" Debbie asked.

"Maybe later," I grumbled then walked into the room and almost dove for the bed; shoes on and all.

In no time at all, I was out.

And in no time at all, I was back to the easy life.

The life when I had money, women, luxuries, and anything else I wanted.

When I was a criminal.

I was on the computer with my buddies one day looking up credit card information to steal. One particular person's information we stole, I happened to remember his name. It was a Simon and the last name began with an H. It was Hartman or Hartford or something like that. Then something came to me right there. The Simon I knew, his last name was Hardy.

Could it be that...?

I'm sorry, buddy.

Then I woke up in a cold sweat. I looked at the clock. It had 9:05 p.m.

Damn! I was late.

I immediately jumped up, changed my clothes, grabbed my car keys and my work keys and I was on my way. I walked into the living room to see Debbie sitting on the couch with her head tilted and her eyes closed.

She still had the remote in her hand. I went back into the room and on the dresser, I saw that Tupac CD Simon bought me. I thought, "Can't leave without this."

But that's not what I came back for. I then got the blanket off of the bed and walked back into the living room and covered Debbie up.

Then I left.

When I got in the car, I decided not to listen to any music, but just to focus on getting there soon without speeding.

Soon enough, I was there.

I got out of the car, but when I did, a very cool gust of wind hit me and sent a chill through my body. I said to myself, "That's odd on a summer's night like this." I thought nothing of it and went into the building.

I walked in, locked the door behind me, and turned the lights on. Then I immediately got started.

I decided to start with the windows first. I went into the closet and grabbed the window cleaner and a few rags.

I started on the left side and worked my way around.

When I was done doing that, I polished all of the stainless steel.

Then I began on the floor. Just as I was finishing mopping the floor, I happened to look up from the floor to see a man standing by the door and then he began walking towards me. I was shocked because I could've sworn I locked the door.

"Hey buddy, there's not supposed to be anyone but me in here at this time of night. Plus how'd you get in here? I know I locked that door."

"You did," the man replied. "But locks don't work on me. You see, I'm the Devil."

FIFTEEN

I thought I heard him say he was the Devil, but I was sure that that wasn't what he said so I asked, "You said you're who?"

"You heard me right, Henry. I'm the Devil."

There he stood right in front of me. Something about his very presence gave me that same chill I got before coming in.

Then the first thing to pop into my mind was Simon. Simon put this guy up to this as a practical joke. But then looking at him closer, he looked as if he were a little high. Finally, I concluded that this guy was just crazy.

"No, Simon didn't put me up to this, no I'm not high, and no I'm not crazy."

My eyes did a double-take. How'd he know exactly what I was just thinking?

But back to reality.

"That was pretty good and I don't know how you knew what I was thinking, but you're going to have to leave," I said getting irritated with his tricks.

"No tricks, Henry. I am who I say I am."

"Alright, Devil or no Devil, you still have to leave," I said still believing this guy just escaped from the crazy house.

I put my hand on his shoulder to help direct him out. As soon as I did, I saw a spark where my hand was and I felt a burn on my palm and saw steam come from his shoulder.

"I let myself in and I can let myself out," he calmly said.

I looked at my palm tending to the burn that seared my skin. When I looked up to face him again, he was gone.

As if no one were ever there in the first place.

Where'd this guy go?

Was there anyone there anyway?

I must be losing my mind.

Then I thought to just yesterday when I was so tired and how little sleep I got.

I really should get more sleep.

At that point, I didn't worry about finishing mopping. I hurried and put the mop in the closet. I didn't dump the water out of the mop bucket, but left it there. I then headed for the door and turned the lights out and left. I locked the door behind me.

Then I got to the car.

On the way home, I was thinking to myself, "Who was this guy? More importantly, how'd he get in if I'm the only one with the key?"

But then I noticed something. I touched his shoulder with my right hand. And that was the hand that got burned. But then driving right now with my right hand on the steering wheel, I feel no pain. So I looked at my palm and there was not a single mark.

So it was all in my mind.

Man, I tell you when I get home, I'm going straight to bed and sleep long and hard and get all the rest I need.

Before long I was at home.

When I walked in, I saw Debbie lying on the couch underneath a blanket resting with her head on a pillow.

I figured if she would go through all that trouble to get comfortable, why didn't she just go lie in the bed in the bedroom where she could stretch out more.

Well it doesn't matter. Just means more room for me in bed.

I went in and got into my night clothes and hopped in bed.

I slept and slept until I felt a finger stroking my cheek. I awakened to see Debbie sitting on the bed caressing my face.

"Wake up, honey. Time for breakfast."

She then took my hand – my right hand. I jumped back at the pain. I looked at it and it was full of huge blisters.

I thought I was still dreaming.

SIXTEEN

"Oh my God, Henry! What happened to your hand?" she said in a startled voice.

"I don't know," I said in a half-whisper. "I thought it was a dream or hallucination."

"Well that doesn't look like a dream or hallucination. That looks very real and like it deserves medical attention."

"And what am I going to tell them, Debbie? That I don't know how this got here. The doctor's going to look at me like I'm nuts."

"Well why don't you start by telling me what you do know?"

"Alright. So late last night I was working and I see this guy in the building. I had no idea how he got in because I locked the door like I always do. Then he says he's the Devil. So my first notion is either Simon put this guy up to this or he's high on somethin'. I told him to leave and put my hand on his shoulder to show him the way out. Then I saw a spark of fire where my hand was and then steam. I looked down at my hand, but when I looked back up he was gone."

When I got done talking, I saw the look on Debbie's face. The disbelief was obvious.

"Please Deb, you gotta believe me. Do you think I would make this up?"

"I just think you need more sleep. You know, sometimes things happen when we're tired and we don't always remember how it happened."

"Maybe you're right."

"So you say you saw the Devil?" Debbie inquired in a mocking tone.

"So you think this is funny?"

"Actually it is a little funny," she said.

"Yeah, maybe a little," I replied and then we both burst out laughing at the same time.

"So can we put all this behind us and get some breakfast? I made your favorite," she said rubbing my arm.

"That sounds great, honey," I said. Then we went to the kitchen for breakfast.

Once breakfast was over, I was half-way done washing the dishes when the doorbell rang.

"I'll get it," Debbie announced and then went to the living room.

"Who is it?" I called from the kitchen.

I didn't get a response so I went into the living room. When I got there, I didn't see anyone in the living room, but the front door was open some. I walked up and heard Debbie talking to Simon.

"Well I think he should just rest for today. He really needs his sleep. He's starting to imagine things from a lack of sleep and it's bothering me."

I coughed to alert them of my presence. "Hey Simon," I said making it look as if I just got there.

"Oh hey, buddy. How ya doin'?"

"Oh not too good. Last night some crazy dude was in the warehouse with me. He tried to spook me by telling me he was the Devil. You know anything about that?"

"No," Simon said looking from Debbie to me. "Why would I?"

"Alright Simon, how much?"

"How much what?"

"How much did you pay this guy to pull this prank?"

"Henry, I swear to you I didn't put anyone up to this."

The look on Simon's face let me know that he had nothing to do with this nor did he know what I was talking about.

"Well if it wasn't you, Simon, that could mean only one thing. I didn't lock the door when I thought I locked it and this lunatic comes strolling in."

So we can rule out the option of a practical joke.

Still thinking of possible answers as to what it was that happened last night, I turned to go back into the house.

"Where you goin', buddy? You haven't been out here five minutes."

"To get more rest."

SEVENTEEN

As I slept uncomfortably in my bed, I dreamed. I dreamed of my entire life up to the point of last night when this man with slick black hair and a smooth baby face tells me he's the Devil.

Then I woke up.

I looked at the clock and it said 8:43 p.m.

I must've really been sleeping hard.

As soon as I sat up, I felt my stomach in knots from a lack of food.

I was starving.

Where was Debbie and why hadn't she woke me up?

I got up and went to the kitchen and straight to the refrigerator. On the refrigerator door was a note that read, "You seemed so tired, I just decided to let you sleep. I bought you a couple of burgers from Wendy's.

Deb."

I opened the refrigerator to see a Wendy's bag sitting there. I pulled it out. Realizing I had to hurry so I could get to work, I rushed to the microwave and put the bag in and set it for thirty seconds. When it was done, I pulled the bag out and opened it and pulled the two burgers out. They were still somewhat cold, but I figured, "What the hell?" and opened up one and began to indulge. They were both Jr. Bacon Cheeseburgers. I was eating them quickly so as not to waste time when I heard a voice in the living room. Thinking it was the T.V., I continued eating. Then I heard the voice again and it sounded like Debbie's voice. When I heard it a third time, I was sure it was Debbie.

But who was she talking to?

I went into the living room to see Debbie curled up on the couch with a blanket on her.

She was sleep.

On the T.V. screen was Matthew Broderick. I recognized the movie immediately – "Ferris Beuller's Day Off." Lately it had become routine for her to fall asleep while watching a movie.

Then she started talking again.

"Henry, Henry honey. I really do love you more than anything," she cried out still sleeping.

"I love you too, babe," I said in a half-whisper. I looked at the clock by the lamp.

I had to hurry.

I ran to the bathroom, washed up real quick, changed my clothes, and in a few minutes I was out the door.

When I got in the car, before I put the key in the ignition, I thought to myself, "This guy better not show up tonight." Then I thought, "Of course he won't if you make sure you lock the damn door."

I put the key in the ignition, started the car up, and before long I was there.

Then I got out of the car and went in. As soon as I got in, the first thing I did was lock the door. Then I double-checked to make sure it was locked.

Satisfied that no one was getting through that door tonight, I began work.

The more I worked, the more I forgot about this guy and the less worried I became.

But why was I worried?

Soon, after so much work, I came to the last part – the floor.

I was just getting done sweeping and about to make mop water to mop my floor when I heard a voice say, "Are you afraid of me, Henry?"

I jerked my head around so fast, I nearly broke my neck.

There he was. Same guy.

Only this time, he was a few feet away from me.

A drop of sweat fell from my forehead. I hadn't realized I was sweating till that point.

"Henry, I can understand your fears and doubts."

His voice was so mellow.

I was finally able to muster up a few words.

"Look, I don't know who you are or what you want, but enough's enough."

"Henry, let me tell you this. You are a faith-goer. You live by faith and the word of the Lord. Doesn't the word teach you that Satan is real?"

"Yeah, but I know better enough to know that you ain't Him. Now you've got three seconds to turn around and walk out that door and never come back."

"I'm not leaving."

"Alright, let's say you are the Devil," I said trying to humor myself. "What do you want from me?"

"It's actually nothing I want from you. It's Debbie I'm after."

EIGHTEEN

"What the hell did you say?" I asked.

"You heard me right, Henry. It's not you I'm after. It's Debbie."

"Wait, how the hell do you know my wife's name, you son-of-a bitch?" I said balding my fist up and then taking a swing.

But right before my very eyes, he dematerialized, and my fist went right through the spot he was standing.

"I'm right behind you," I heard that calm voice say followed by a tap on my shoulder.

I swiveled around to see him standing there.

Is this what losing your mind is like?

"I don't know how you did that, but try dodging this," I said balding my fist up again ready to try for another swing.

He then put up his left hand as if signaling me to stop. "Trying to harm me is useless," he responded. "Just hear what I have to say."

"Alright buddy, you got fifteen seconds," I said lowering my fist. "Spit it out."

"Alright Henry. It's not you at all I'm after. It's Debbie. No, you're not losing your mind because I can assure you I'm real. You have changed your life and have stayed on the path of God and you followed the word. Debbie has changed over her life to following God as well. But unlike you, she has not been able to stick close to God. You know all those times when you were trying to get her to study and grow in the word of God with you, she seemed distant and uninterested? That was her losing the faith. And now because her lack of faith has grown so much, she now lacks the faith necessary to keep me from taking her soul."

"If you harm my wife..." I said balding my fist up to punch him in the face.

Suddenly the lights went off for one second, then came back on. He was gone.

"I'm coming for her, Henry. And believe me, I'll get her," I heard a faint whisper say.

I suddenly felt light-headed. Then I saw all black. The next thing I knew, what seemed like a few seconds later, I felt someone lightly slapping my face.

"Henry, Henry, you O.K.?" I heard a voice say.

I opened my eyes to see the guys from the day crew standing around me.

My God, what happened?

I stood up to see the sunlight beaming through the windows.

"Where is he?! Where is that bastard?!" I yelled.

The other guys just stood there looking at me.

"Who?" one of them finally spoke up. "It's just us here."

I began turning my head, left to right, then behind me to see if I could find him. I then saw Bill standing at the office door. He sadly shook his head and walked into the office. I walked to the office and walked in.

"Bill, where the hell is he?"

"Who?"

"This guy that says he's the Devil."

"Now Henry, you know I think you're a great worker. And if you need some time off, you know I'll give you that. But you know I don't allow drugs on my premises."

"Aw, to hell with drugs! I don't do any drugs. I'm tellin' you this guy keeps comin' in when the doors are locked and tellin' me he's the Devil."

"I'm not doubting you," Bill said with his mouth fixed in an obvious expression of disbelief.

"Dammit Bill, I'm not crazy!"

"No one is saying you are," Bill calmly said. "Look, we'll be watching out for him all day. If he shows up, we'll turn him over to the police for trespassing. In the meantime, you go home and get some rest."

"Yeah, that sounds like a good idea."

With that, I left.

NINETEEN

"Debbie... Debbie, I'm home," I said closing the front door. As soon as I did, there was that great aroma.

Debbie cooked my special meal.

I walked into the kitchen to see her at the stove hard at work – she didn't have anything on but a t-shirt and a pair of panties.

I walked up behind her and wrapped my arms around her waist.

"Hey handsome," she said without looking at me.

"Hey babe," I said with my arms still hugging her waist. "How ya doin'?"

"A lot better now that you're here. By the way, why'd you work so late?"

Here I'm faced with an option. Either tell her the truth that this guy that calls himself the Devil showed up again last night and said that he's really not interested in me at all, but is really after her soul, and I blacked out and when I came to, it was daytime and the guys from the day crew had to wake me up, or I could just lie to her.

I chose option one because she deserves the truth. I owe her that much.

"Well Deb," I began, "I saw that guy again last night." She started to say something, but I cut her off.

"Just hear me out," I began again. "He told me the reason he keeps popping up has nothing to do with me. He says he's after you."

She gave a startled expression. "Me?"

"Yes. He says by you growing so distant from the Bible is due to the fact that you're losing your faith. He says and now it's to the point where you have lost so much faith that you lack the faith necessary to keep him from taking your soul."

I looked at her and studied her for a reaction, but I couldn't find what I was looking for.

"Well, I hope you straightened him out," she finally retorted.

"Yeah honey, I did," I lied. "When I got done with him, he said he was never coming back."

"But on a bad note, the guys think I'm crazy and Bill thinks I'm on drugs. Bill thinks I need more rest."

"That's not what you need."

"Oh really, and what do I need?"

"All you need is sexual healing," she said singing the 'Sexual Healing' song by Marvin Gaye while holding my hands and leading me to the bedroom.

"Well, let's get it on," I said singing the 'Let's get it on' song by Marvin Gaye also.

Then we went in the bedroom and closed the door.

TWENTY

"I'm coming for her, Henry. And believe me, I'll get her," I heard that calm voice say. I jumped up in a cold sweat.

"Debbie!" I screamed.

I looked around and realized I had just woke up from a bad dream. But then it occurred to me – I had to use the bathroom. As I was getting out of bed to go to the bathroom, I heard a noise. It was a very static-like noise that appeared to be coming from the living room. As I approached the living room, the noise got louder. When I got to the living room, I saw the T.V. on, but there was nothing on but the static that lets you know the shows have gone off. And there was Debbie curled up on the couch underneath a blanket sleeping.

Suddenly, without her moving a muscle, I heard her say, "Henry, why did you let him get me? You were supposed to protect me, Henry. I don't understand. Haven't I been good to you? But you still let him get me."

Then she sat up and without her body moving at all, her head turned around and I could see her extra pale skin like a ghost.

I felt my heart racing a mile a minute. Then she jumped up from the couch and started towards me. I turned to run back to the bedroom. I ran in, slammed the door shut, and hopped in bed and pulled the covers over my head.

I heard the footsteps approaching the bedroom door – THUMP, THUMP, THUMP!

Then I heard the beating on the door as she cried out, "Henry, I thought I had been good to you."

Then the door swung open and I hopped up in another cold sweat.

This time it was daylight. But I wasn't taking any chances. I pinched my elbow and then my bicep hoping to feel the pain and that way I'd know I was awake. I felt the sting of both pinches.

But I had to be sure.

So I slapped myself in the face and when I felt that, I was satisfied.

I got up and made my way to the kitchen. I was thirsty as hell.

When I got to the kitchen, I opened the refrigerator up and took the orange juice out. I took the top off and turned it up.

I didn't need a cup.

I kept drinking and drinking till it was all gone. As I was throwing the bottle away, I noticed there was a note on the table. I picked it up:

Henry,

I noticed we're getting low on food again, so Simon was nice enough to take me grocery shopping. I won't be gone long.

Deb.

"Alright," I said to myself and then went to take my shower.

When I was done with my shower and was dressed, I decided to wait for Debbie to come home. So I sat on the couch and about an hour and a half later, I heard the key turn inside of the front door. Debbie came in and Simon followed.

"Hey buddy," Simon announced. "Man, you missed the best pizza ever."

"Pizza?" I inquired.

"Yeah, me and Deb went out for lunch."

That's not what the note said.

"Debbie, you said you guys were going shopping."

"We did," Simon piped up, "but afterwards we got a little hungry."

But not only that, but there were no bags of any groceries with them.

"So where are the groceries, Simon?"

'You know we just couldn't find what we were looking for," Simon responded.

"I understand," I said.

TWENTY-ONE

I knew Bill didn't believe me, the guys at work didn't believe me, and Simon nor Debbie believed me.

Hell, I didn't believe me!

But I was determined to catch that bastard and make someone believe me.

So I put the recorder in my pocket and made sure the batteries worked O.K.

Then I was ready to go.

On the way there, all I could think about was this guy and what I would say to him. Almost as if that were the only reason I was going, and not to work at all.

Before long, I was there.

When I got out of the car, I felt in my pocket to make sure I had my tape recorder.

Then I went in.

When I got in, I flipped the lights on and went to the nearest chair to wait for his arrival. I purposely didn't lock the door so as to make it as easy as possible for him to come in.

There I sat for a few hours – just waiting. Finally I decided, "This is ridiculous. He was probably just some deranged guy and you already scared him off. I should really get some work done."

I got up to go lock the doors.

Just as I turned the key in the lock, I heard that voice say, "I take it you were waiting for me?"

I looked behind me and there he was sitting in the chair I was just sitting in.

I got you now, you son-of-a bitch. I slid my hand inside of my pocket where the recorder was and hit the record button.

As I approached him, I called out, "Who are you and what do you want?"

"I told you, Henry. I'm the Devil and I'm after Debbie."

"Suppose you plan on tellin' me just how you're going to get her."

"I'm Satan. I can get anything I want."

"And you say you're who?" I said leaning closer to him to make sure the recorder picked it up.

"I told you. I'm the Devil. I'm surprised you don't believe in me."

"Oh, I believe in the Devil. But just not that you're him."

"I know exactly what you believe in, Henry. I know things about you that you don't even know. I've been watching you a long time."

"You mean you've been stalking me?"

"No, not at all. Let me explain. You see, life is a test – a very simple test. In the end, those that follow the word of God and walk in His path are protected from me and they go to Heaven. Those that don't, go to Hell. It's that simple. You already know that. But what you didn't know is that both God and I watch everyone. We both know everything about everyone. With this ever-so simple test of life and faith, those who deviate from God's path, for whatever reason, He gives me permission to take them. Whereas you still walk in the light of God and follow His word, Debbie no longer does. She has lost the faith. Which is why I'm here to collect what is mine."

"You better not lay one finger on my wife, you bastard!" I exclaimed balding my fist up and swinging for his face. But he dematerialized and I hit the chair – hard.

So hard I put a dent in it.

I looked around me to see if I could see him, but he was gone.

"Time is ticking, Henry," I heard his voice say.

"Oh and Henry, recorders don't work on the voice of darkness."

It was then that I pulled out the recorder and hit rewind and then play.

When I heard his voice on there with everything he had just said, I said to myself, "We'll see about that one."

TWENTY-TWO

After that lunatic left, I decided to wait for the crew to get there in the morning. I had evidence so they could see I wasn't crazy.

Here I stood with the entire crew around me with Bill at the forefront of the guys. I had the recorder in my hand and I had just got done telling them what took place in there last night.

"So everything he said is right here," I said hitting the play button.

I expected to hear his voice just like after he left and I heard it on the recorder. Instead it was just a fuzzy static sound.

"What the hell?" I said shaking it up as if that would get it working again.

I heard some giggling going on, but when I looked up to see who it was, I saw a few of the guys trying to compose themselves as if they weren't laughing.

"I tell you, Bill, I heard him on here as plain as day," I said as I continuously hit rewind and play.

I looked up to see Bill looking at me with the saddest expression is his eyes.

Then Bill motioned me away from the crowd and talked to me in a low tone where only I could hear.

"You know, Henry, I was thinking maybe the night shift might be a bit too much for you. Why don't you consider coming back to the day crew where we can all be around you?"

He saw the look on my face and then got ready to counter my anger.

"Look, no one is calling you crazy. And no one is denying that this guy keeps coming in and saying what you said he said. Only thing is, no one is seeing this guy but you. But at least if you were on the day shift, we could all be here to catch him together."

"Maybe you're right," I said sensing that Bill still thought I was crazy. But so as not to start any static, I went along with it.

"That doesn't sound like a bad idea. Maybe I will go back to the day shift. But for now I just need some rest," I said turning to leave.

"Now you're talking," Bill happily exclaimed.

I walked past the guys and through the front door. When I got outside, I pulled the recorder out, rewinded it, and hit play. And then I heard his voice on there saying what he said last night.

"I tell you, Debbie, I got that son-of-a bitch's voice on the recorder if you'd take a moment to listen," I said following her into the living room.

"If it didn't work for Bill and the guys, why would it work now?"

"I told you, I heard it plain as day once I got outside. Deb, I'm not crazy. Just give me a moment."

"Alright, alright," she said sitting on the couch. I sat next to her and with the recorder in hand, I hit rewind.

"Are you ready?" I said preparing her.

"As ready as I'll get."

Then I hit play. All we could hear was a static sound.

"Damn, this stupid thing!" I shouted.

"Henry dear," she began placing her hand on my ear and rubbing it, "I think it's time we give Dr. Wells a visit."

"No, Debbie. Now you're thinking like Bill."

"Well what other options are there?"

"You could try believing in me."

"Henry, I love you. I really do. But if you need help, then you need help. I'm sure that there's some medication he can give you."

I stood and looked long and hard at Debbie. "You're the one person I can trust," I said. "Why don't you trust me?"

Then, with the recorder, I walked out onto the front porch. I was all alone. I hit rewind and play and there, plain as day, I heard his voice.

This couldn't be possible. Am I losing my mind?

Maybe it is time we give Dr. Wells a visit.

TWENTY-THREE

The only other option I could think of would be to quit my job and check into the nearest mental institution. Who else sees people and has conversations with people that aren't there?

Then it hit me.

Maybe he was there.

And maybe he is the Devil.

One thing's for sure, if he is the Devil then it's futile trying to hide from him in a mental institution. He'll just keep showing up wherever you go.

It was then and there I decided Devil or no Devil, I'm not hiding from anyone. My mom didn't raise a coward.

So I'll work my shift again tonight and if I see this guy again, I'll just ignore him.

"Are you sure you're ready?"

"Yep, I'm ready."

"And you have everything you need?"

"All I need is this," I said pointing to my temple signifying that all I needed was my mind.

"Alright, babe," Debbie said leaning in for a kiss. "Love you."

"I love you too, honey."

"Have a good night."

"Bye."

"Bye."

With that, I left.

I told Debbie all I needed was my mind. Little did she know I had a little something extra for him.

When I got to the car, I got in. Then I pulled it out – the gun Simon gave me.

I'll teach you to threaten my wife, you bastard.

Then I put it on the seat next to me and drove to work.

When I got there, I was so anxious to deal with this guy I went in the warehouse and didn't even lock the car door.

The first thing I did was turn the lights on. Soon as I did, they started flickering on and off.

And I could feel his presence.

"Come out, you motherfucker! I know you're here!" I screamed.

"I'm right here," I heard that mellow voice say followed by a tap on my shoulder.

I swiveled around to see him standing right there.

"Aha!" I exclaimed. "I got somethin' for you."

I then hurriedly pulled the gun out and let him have it.

BANG! BANG! BANG!

Each shot hit him directly in the chest. He fell over onto the floor and when he didn't move, I'd figured I'd killed him.

So far the plan was going smoothly.

Next I went to the closet and got out a pair of plastic gloves and put them on so there wouldn't be any fingerprints. Then I dragged his body to my car, opened the trunk and threw him in. Then I drove to the river.

It was about a thirty minute drive but well worth it.

I opened the trunk, pulled his lifeless body out, and hoisted him into the river. I just stood there a second and watched his lifeless body flow with the current. Then I hopped back in my car and headed for the warehouse.

When I got there, I put the bloody gloves in my trunk and went in to finish my shift.

When I went in, I turned on the lights – no flickering.

I went to the closet to get the window cleaner so I could start on the windows.

Then I heard that mellow voice say, "I'm surprised you think that bullets would work on the Prince of Darkness."

I turned totally around to see him standing there – not a mark on him. He was as clean as ever.

I couldn't believe it.

I fell back, knocking over the mop bucket and landing on the floor.

With my eyes wide and staring at him, I said, "I saw you die. I threw you in the river."

"Now do you believe I am who I say I am?"

"This guy really is the Devil," I whispered to myself.

TWENTY-FOUR

As he began to advance towards me, I could feel the fear rising in me.

Then he said, "I can feel your fear. But as I told you before, you have nothing to worry about. It's not you I'm after. It's Debbie."

I still felt very afraid. Although I wasn't sure if this fear was for me or Debbie.

"But I saw you die."

"Henry, you can't kill Satan with a gun. I'm immortal. I thought you knew better. Now do you believe I am who I say I am?"

Surprisingly I began to calm down.

"Let's say you are the Devil and you're after Debbie, is there anything I can do to stop you?"

"Maybe."

Then, as if snapping back to reality, I thought to myself, "Listen to you. You're actually believing and going along with this guy. Enough is enough!" I said feeling around my pockets.

"Looking for this?" he announced holding up my gun.

"Give that back to me."

"Of course," he said tossing it to me.

Immediately after catching it, I wasted no time with aiming the gun at him and pulling the trigger.

BANG! BANG!

I saw the bullets penetrate him, but then he smiled and began to advance towards me.

"When will you learn?"

Soon he was right in front of me. He bent down and took the gun out of my hand. He then bent the gun into nothingness before my very eyes.

I was in awe.

"Henry, this is very unproductive. I just want to talk to you."

"About what?" I said fully convinced that he was the Devil.

"About saving your wife's soul."

"Forget it."

"Maybe you need a little more proof for you to believe I am the Devil so you'll hear me out. This won't hurt at all," he said coming closer to me.

I knew he was about to lay hands on me, yet somehow I believed when he said it wouldn't hurt.

He put two of his fingers to my right temple and then said, "Close your eyes."

I did so.

When I did, I saw myself as a little boy. I was sitting on the floor late one night watching T.V. because daddy said I could stay up a little later that night. Mom wasn't home yet. When she did finally come home, the two of them got into a big argument. Daddy accused her of staying out late having an affair. She tried to tell him she was looking for a job. She then told me to go to my room and go to bed. I told her daddy said I could stay up late. But she insisted that I go to bed. I didn't understand why she wouldn't let me watch T.V. I went to my room and went to bed and mommy and daddy went to theirs. As I slept that night, I remember feeling so much anger and hatred towards mom for not letting me stay up late when daddy already said I could. I figured she did it to hurt my feelings.

Then the truth hit me.

That night, when mommy and daddy went into their room, he raped her and she knew he was going to do it so by telling me to go to bed, she was making sure I was out of harm's way.

She was protecting me.

I'm sorry, mommy.

Then I began to see other events in my life where the truth was revealed right there with the Devil.

The last thing he showed me was when I was on my computer at my house with my friends stealing information from people's credit cards.

Then I saw something I had never seen. I saw my friends talking one time about telling the police about my criminal activity on-line so they could get all of my share of wealth I had accumulated when I went to jail.

"Those bastards," I murmured.

"Have you seen enough?" I heard the Devil say removing his fingers from my temple.

"O.K. I'm convinced."

"Very good. And I think you should know I'll be coming for her tomorrow night."

TWENTY-FIVE

When I got home, I walked into the kitchen and saw Debbie sitting at the table drinking a cup of coffee.

"Hey honey," I announced.

"Hey babe," she responded. "Did you see that lunatic again?"

I felt it better not to tell her anything that happened. "No, I guess he got scared."

"So can we finally put all this behind us and move on?"

"I don't see why not. I decided to take tonight off to be with you."

"That's great. Did you have any plans of going anywhere special tonight?"

"No, just a nice quiet evening with my wife."

I looked at the clock and it said 8:02 p.m. I figured I'd get the trash ready and taken out tonight so the trash man could get it in the morning.

Debbie was in the kitchen.

Before I got the trash ready, I asked Debbie to cook my special meal of hashbrowns, scrambled eggs, bacon, toast, and a cup of coffee. While she was cooking it, I got the trash ready to go out. I got it all together and before I walked out the back door, I looked at Debbie with the most loving eyes and said, "I love you, babe."

She then responded, "O.K., I love you too. But where did that come from?"

Then, with the trash bags in my hands, I walked out.

I prepared Henry's meal. Then I sat there. I thought about everything Henry had been telling me about this guy that calls himself the Devil. Then I thought about what Henry said he was after me.

Then it hit me like a rock in the head.

The teachings Henry was trying to teach me about in the Bible of the sacrificial lamb. The sacrificing of one for the good of others.

Sacrificial lamb!

Now as I sat there contemplating this, I noticed that Henry's hashbrowns had grown hard, the scrambled eggs had become cold, the bacon had lost its crispiness, the toast was no longer soft, and the coffee had grown cold and weak.

Then I thought about that far off look Henry had in his eyes as he said, "I love you" when taking the trash out.

That was forty minutes ago.

Henry's not coming back.

EPILOGUE

When Henry went out the back door with the bags of trash, he met with the Devil and sacrificed his soul for Debbie's. That was the sacrificial lamb. As for Simon and Debbie, they moved in together. They were having an affair anyway. Then one day on the way home from work, an eighteen-wheeler hit Simon's car on the intersection. He died. Then Debbie went back to her previous life of prostitution. Sometime later, she contracted AIDS and in no time at all, she was dead. So this is the fate of Henry, Debbie, and Simon. All three of them are in hell.

AFTERWORD

In the introduction, it was stated that growing up, I very heavily believed in and relied on science to provide answers to the different mysteries of the world. I did not have that faith or belief in God for such inquiries. The bible teaches us about both heaven and hell. At one point in my life, I devised my own idea of what heaven and hell are if they do in fact exist.

I analyzed the fact that when people die, it is something like a deep sleep from which you never awake. Your soul lives on, but in a perpetual dream-like state. In this state you still experience some form of life. This could be considered the afterlife.

This afterlife can be good – heaven, or bad – hell. It all depends on what kind of dream you are having in this perpetual state. My thoughts were that if it's a good dream that you are experiencing, then you are in the place called heaven. And just the opposite, if you are experiencing a bad dream, then it's hell.

Once you are in a state of death, you never wake up from this dream like you do in the morning.

It's forever.